Dear Parents and Educators,

Welcome to Penguin Young Readers! As parents and educators, you know that each child develops at his or her own pace—in terms of speech, critical thinking, and, of course, reading. Penguin Young Readers recognizes this fact. As a result, each Penguin Young Readers book is assigned a traditional easy-to-read level (1–4) as well as a Guided Reading Level (A–P). Both of these systems will help you choose the right book for your child. Please refer to the back of each book for specific leveling information. Penguin Young Readers features esteemed authors and illustrators, stories about favorite characters, fascinating nonfiction, and more!

Mo Jackson: Get a Hit, Mo!

LEVEL **2**

GUIDED READING LEVEL **I**

This book is perfect for a **Progressing Reader** who:
- can figure out unknown words by using picture and context clues;
- can recognize beginning, middle, and ending sounds;
- can make and confirm predictions about what will happen in the text; and
- can distinguish between fiction and nonfiction.

Here are some **activities** you can do during and after reading this book:

- Adding -ing to Words: One of the rules when adding -ing to words is, when a word ends with an -e, take off the -e and add -ing. With other words, you simply add the -ing ending to the root word. The following words are -ing words in this story: playing, losing, cheering, shouting, standing, rolling, running. On a separate piece of paper, write down the root word for each of the words.
- Make Connections: In this story, Mo has a hard time hitting the ball. But he still manages to win the game for his team. Have you ever had trouble with something? How did it make you feel? What did you do to get better at it?

Remember, sharing the love of reading with a child is the best gift you can give!

—Sarah Fabiny, Editorial Director
Penguin Young Readers program

*Penguin Young Readers are leveled by independent reviewers applying the standards developed by Irene Fountas and Gay Su Pinnell in *Matching Books to Readers: Using Leveled Books in Guided Reading*, Heinemann, 1999.

For My Little League Grandsons
Jacob, Yoni, Andrew, and Aaron—DAA

For Enoch—SR

PENGUIN YOUNG READERS
An Imprint of Penguin Random House LLC

The Library of Congress has cataloged the hardcover edition under the following Control Number: 2015028485

ISBN 9780448480107   10 9

GET A HIT, MO!

by David A. Adler
illustrated by Sam Ricks

Penguin Young Readers
An Imprint of Penguin Random House

"Bam!" Mo Jackson says.

He swings a carrot stick.

"Bam!" he says again.

"It is a home run."

Bam! Bam! Bam!

"Finish your snack,"

Mo's father tells him.

"It is almost time to go."

Mo swings the carrot stick

one more time.

Then he eats it.

Mo's parents take him
to the baseball field.
Mo's team is the Lions.
Today the Lions are
playing the Bears.

Mo is smaller than the others
on his team.
He is younger, too.

Coach Marie tells the team
when each player will bat.
She tells them where to play
in the field.

Mo will bat last.
I always bat last,
Mo thinks.

He will play right field.

I always play right field, Mo thinks.

No balls ever come to right field.

"Play ball!" the umpire calls.

Mo stands in right field.

He watches the Bears

score two runs.

The Lions are up.

Mo sits on the bench.

He watches his team bat.

He also watches the pitcher.

Whoosh!

Whoosh!

That pitcher throws fast,

Mo thinks.

How will I get a hit?

The Lions don't score.

Mo's team is losing, 2–0.

It is the end of the second inning.

It is Mo's turn to bat.

Whoosh!

"Strike one," the umpire calls.

"Mo! Mo!" Coach Marie shouts.

"Stand close to the plate."

Mo stands close to the plate.

Whoosh!

"Strike two."

"Mo! Mo!" Coach Marie shouts.

"Swing the bat."

Whoosh!

Mo swings the bat.

He swings too late.

"Strike three," the umpire calls.

"You are out."

Mo stands in right field.

He watches the other

team's batters.

When the ball is too high or too low,

they don't swing.

When the ball is just right,

they swing and hit the ball.

That's what I'll do, Mo thinks.

In the fourth inning

it's Mo's turn to bat again.

When the ball is just right,

Mo swings.

But he swings too late.

Mo strikes out again.

I want to hit a home run,

Mo thinks.

But all I do is strike out.

It is the last inning.

There are two outs.

Mo may be the last batter
of the game.

People are cheering.

Coach Marie is shouting.

Mo can't hear Coach Marie.

Whoosh!

"Strike one,"

the umpire calls.

The cheering gets louder.

Coach Marie shouts louder.

Mo still can't hear her.

Whoosh!

"Strike two."

One more strike and
the game is over.
People are standing.
People are cheering.

Mo turns to hear what

Coach Marie is shouting.

When he turns,

his bat turns, too.

Crack!

The ball hits Mo's bat.

The ball rolls quickly past
the pitcher.

"Run! Run!" Coach Marie
and other Lions shout.

Mo runs.

He gets to first base.

The ball keeps rolling.

"Run! Run!"

Mo keeps running.

He runs to second base.

The two Lions who were on base score.

"We win! We win!" Coach Marie

and others shout.

The Lions run to Mo.

Mo's parents run, too.

"This time, I didn't strike out,"
Mo says.

Coach Marie says, "This time
you won the game."